The SLEEPY PUPPY

Written by Michèle Dufresne

Pioneer Valley Educational Press, Inc.

I am sleeping

on the floor.

2

I am sleeping

on the pillow.

I am sleeping

on the rug.

I am sleeping

on the couch.

I am sleeping

on the bed.

11

I am sleeping
on my dad.